This scene is showing when
the boat was speeding
next to an alligator. I
chose this scene
because when my teacher
read it to me it was the
first thing that popped in to
my head.

farming

This scene is showing the
farm and how well the
farmers did on planting all
these trees and other plants.
I chose this scene because
it would be fun to draw all
these crops.

Speeding
Boat

One Night in the Everglade

In the Everglade

Laurel Larsen, Ph.D.

Illustrated by Joyce Mihran Turley

Moonlight Publishing

TAYLOR TRADE PUBLISHING

Lanham • New York • Boulder • Toronto • Plymouth, UK

Published by
Taylor Trade Publishing
An imprint of
The Rowman & Littlefield Publishing
Group, Inc.
4501 Forbes Boulevard, Suite 200,
Lanham, Maryland 20706
www.rowman.com

Estover Road, Plymouth PL6 7PY, United
Kingdom

Distributed by National Book Network

British Library Cataloguing in Publication
Information Available

Library of Congress Cataloging-in-
Publication Data Available

ISBN 978-0-9817700-4-8 (cloth)
ISBN 978-0-9817700-6-2 (electronic)

♾ ™ The paper used in this publication
meets the minimum requirements
of American National Standard for
Information Sciences—Permanence
of Paper for Printed Library Materials,
ANSI/NISO Z39.48-1992.

Printed in China

Acknowledgments

The production of this book was made possible
through financial support through grants from the
Hubbard Brook Research Foundation, the Southeast
Environmental Research Center's Endowment
supported by the Miccosukee Tribe of Indians and
George Barley funds, and supplementary funding
through the National Science Foundation to the
Florida Coastal Everglades Long Term Ecological
Research program. The advice from D. McKnight
throughout this production and helpful comments
on the content by E. Gaiser and L. Ogden greatly
improved the quality of this book. The children's art
contributed through Pinecrest Elementary School's
Young Friends of the Everglades program and through
Imperial Estates Elementary School is particularly
appreciated and significantly enhanced this book. This
is SERC publication number 518 and a contribution
from the FCE LTER.

About the Long Term Ecological Research (LTER) Network

The National Science Foundation's LTER network
was begun in 1980 and now includes 26 research sites.
The goals of the LTER network are

- Understanding: To understand a diverse array of
ecosystems at multiple spatial and temporal scales.
- Synthesis: To create general knowledge through
long-term, interdisciplinary research, synthesis of
information, and development of theory.
- Information: To inform the LTER and broader
scientific community by creating well designed and
well documented databases.
- Legacies: To create a legacy of well designed and
documented long-term observations, experiments,
and archives of samples and specimens for future
generations.
- Education: To promote training, teaching, and
learning about long-term ecological research and the
Earth's ecosystems, and to educate a new generation
of scientists.
- Outreach: To reach out to the broader scientific
community, natural resource managers,
policymakers, and the general public by providing
decision support, information, recommendations,
and the knowledge and capability to address complex
environmental challenges.

The Schoolyard Series is one component of a broad-
scale, long-term effort to combine scientific research
and science education through the Schoolyard LTER
program. See http://fce.lternet.edu/ and
http://schoolyard.lternet.edu/ for further information.

The

Everglades cover a huge, wet area. Imagine more than 2,261 Olympic-size swimming pools, laid end-to-end. And that distance is the shortest dimension of the Everglades! If instead you were to follow the flow of water from the north tip to the south tip of the Everglades—from Lake Okeechobee to the Florida Bay—you would be flying over the distance of 3,238 Olympic-size pools! In fact, the Everglades have often been called the "river of grass." Some of the water that flows into Lake Okeechobee and the Everglades before entering the Gulf of Mexico comes from as far north as Orlando, Florida—a distance of more than 240 miles!

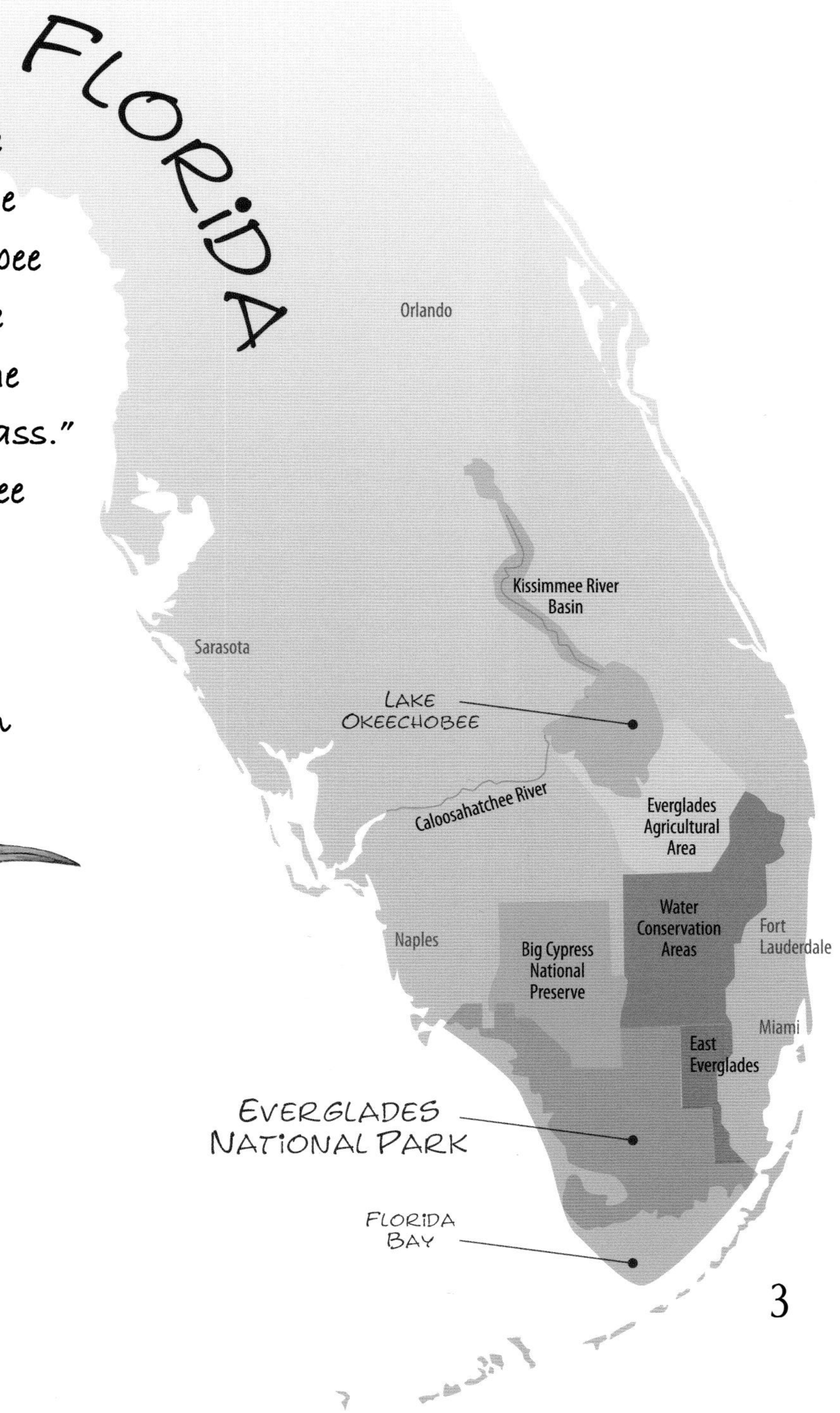

FLORIDA

Orlando

Sarasota

Kissimmee River Basin

Lake Okeechobee

Caloosahatchee River

Everglades Agricultural Area

Water Conservation Areas

East Everglades

Fort Lauderdale

Miami

Everglades

Big Cypress National Preserve

Naples

EVERGLADES NATIONAL PARK

FLORIDA BAY

4

Deep in the Everglades a speeding airboat zips across the water. It races by an alligator as he slides into the water and disappears under a trail of bubbles. A flock of wading white ibises see the boat approach and scatter from where they had been fishing for dinner with their long, curved bills. Among the palm trees in the distance, a rare Florida panther perks up its head at the sound of the roaring engine.

This is the Florida Everglades, home to many animals and plants—some of which can be found nowhere else in the world. That's because there's nowhere else in the world quite like the Everglades, with its miles and miles of shallow marshes, deeper **sloughs** of freshwater, and surprising tree islands that can free float before anchoring in a final spot.

The Everglades is home to some species of tree snails that are found nowhere else in the world. It is also the only place in the U.S. where the beautiful and mysterious ghost orchid is found. It is called the ghost orchid because its stem and roots are difficult to see, making the blossom appear to float in mid-air.

Sloughs: Deeper pools of water in the Everglades that guide the flow of water downstream. Here you will find beautiful white water lilies and gardens of floating purple and yellow flowers.

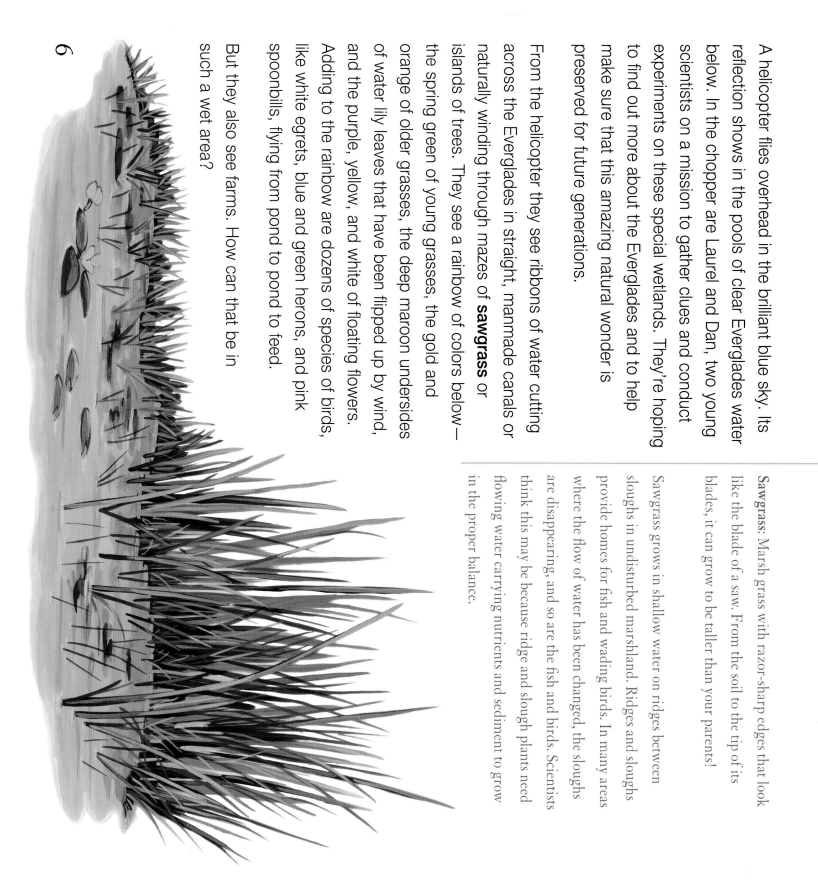

A helicopter flies overhead in the brilliant blue sky. Its reflection shows in the pools of clear Everglades water below. In the chopper are Laurel and Dan, two young scientists on a mission to gather clues and conduct experiments on these special wetlands. They're hoping to find out more about the Everglades and to help make sure that this amazing natural wonder is preserved for future generations.

From the helicopter they see ribbons of water cutting across the Everglades in straight, manmade canals or naturally winding through mazes of **sawgrass** or islands of trees. They see a rainbow of colors below—the spring green of young grasses, the gold and orange of older grasses, the deep maroon undersides of water lily leaves that have been flipped up by wind, and the purple, yellow, and white of floating flowers. Adding to the rainbow are dozens of species of birds, like white egrets, blue and green herons, and pink spoonbills, flying from pond to pond to feed.

But they also see farms. How can that be in such a wet area?

6

Sawgrass: Marsh grass with razor-sharp edges that look like the blade of a saw. From the soil to the tip of its blades, it can grow to be taller than your parents!

Sawgrass grows in shallow water on ridges between sloughs in undisturbed marshland. Ridges and sloughs provide homes for fish and wading birds. In many areas where the flow of water has been changed, the sloughs are disappearing, and so are the fish and birds. Scientists think this may be because ridge and slough plants need flowing water carrying nutrients and sediment to grow in the proper balance.

In the late 1800s, people wanted to use the land in south Florida to grow crops. Since farmers can't grow crops on a wetland, they built canals, which drained water off the Everglades. Then they planted vegetables, oranges, and sugarcane, and grew grass to feed cattle. Pioneers came from all around to settle in the area and become farmers.

Since that time, a system of **pumping stations, canals,** and **levees** has been built to control the flow of water throughout the Everglades. Now there are farms and towns and even whole cities where once there was only wetland. Without these structures working to keep sections of land dry, much of the area would be under water again.

People who live in Florida use water to grow their gardens, fill their bathtubs, and cook their food, just like people anywhere else. All of their water comes from the Everglades, either as surface water that you can see and touch, like in a pond, or as groundwater that you can't see, which is contained deep underground.

Pumping stations: Buildings that control the direction and speed of water flow into or out of Everglades canals.

Canals: Straight, manmade channels for water.

Levees: Long, manmade hills that block the flow of water. Levees are often found alongside canals in the Everglades.

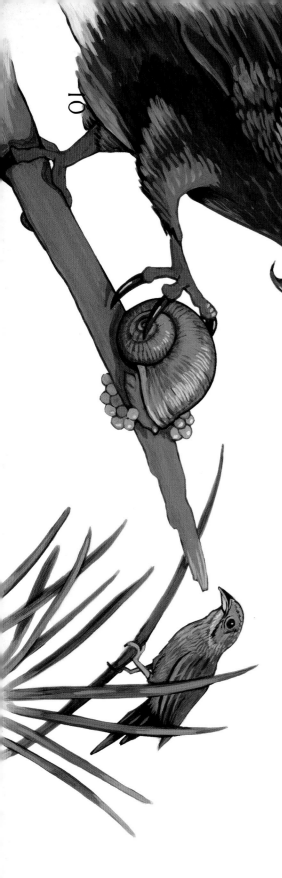

With so much water in the Everglades, early settlers probably never imagined that one day there might not be enough water to go around. But that is something people in Florida are concerned about today. For too long, the canals and levees have been taking too much water away from some parts of the Everglades and flooding other parts with more water than they need.

Some **ecosystems** that existed before humans began building in the Everglades have now disappeared as the flow, timing, and quality of water has been changed. And that means many birds, fish, reptiles, amphibians, mammals, and plants have disappeared as well.

The Everglades is home to 68 **endangered** and threatened species, many of which are in trouble because their habitat is changing. These include the Cape Sable seaside sparrow, which is found primarily in Everglades National Park, and the Florida panther, found primarily in Big Cypress National Preserve. The snail kite, a bird that roams throughout much of the Everglades, is also endangered because the habitat for its main food, the apple snail, is disappearing.

Ecosystem: A community of plants, animals, microscopic organisms, people, and their habitat.

Endangered: A type of plant or animal present on Earth usually in such small numbers that it is in danger of disappearing forever, especially if its habitat is threatened by development or pollution.

A big project is underway to return the Everglades to a more natural state. The project is the biggest, most expensive restoration project in the world, and it will last for at least 30 years. The challenge is: How do you ask an ecosystem how much water it needs? When does it need water? How clean does the water need to be? How fast does it need to be flowing? And what about the stuff that's in the water, called **sediment**? How important is that? Laurel and Dan are part of a team that is working to find out these answers.

But as scientists work to restore the Everglades, they can't forget about the needs of the people who live there, too. Because many communities were built long ago in the Everglades, it's necessary to work to preserve the homes of the people as well as the ecosystems. The goal is to share water between the city dwellers, farmers, plants, and animals of the Everglades.

Laurel knows firsthand the importance of plenty of clean water for the Everglades. She grew up next to a marsh in central Florida, where she loved kayaking and bird-watching. She went to school to become a scientist and got involved in the Everglades restoration project because it was a chance to help preserve one of the most important wetland ecosystems in the world—and also the place she called home.

Since you can't ask a fern or an alligator a question, scientists have other ways of getting answers. Laurel and Dan will be staying up all night in the middle of the Everglades to conduct experiments and gather materials to study back at the lab.

Sediment: Pieces of rock, soil, or plant material deposited at the bottom of lakes, oceans, and rivers, which can be picked up by water currents and carried to other areas.

The Florida Coastal Everglades Long Term Ecological Research (FCE-LTER) project was formed by a group of scientists to study Everglades ecosystems over many years—over a longer period of time than you have been alive!—and to learn how the environment responds to changes.

But first, they must get to their research station in the heart of the marsh. They board an airboat and strap on headphones to protect their hearing from the loud drone of the motor. With a spray of water they shoot off across the marsh. Laurel thinks that riding the airboat feels like flying, and she hangs on tightly.

After they cross the main canal, the marsh grasses stretch before them in all directions, as far as the eye can see. With so much water in sight, it's hard to believe that the Everglades could ever run out of clean water. Yet many areas in the Everglades don't receive water at the right time or in the right amount, or the water's not flowing as quickly as needed. A major goal of the restoration project is to fix these problems for the Everglades ecosystem.

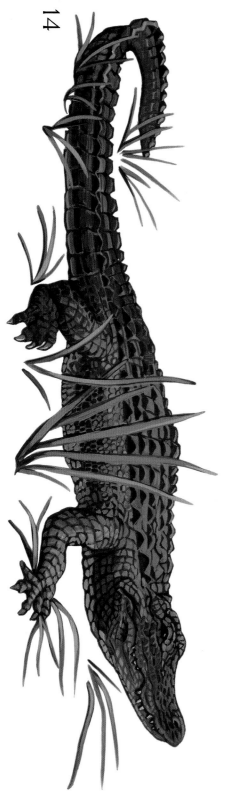

Here is some of the equipment that is on Dan and Laurel's airboat:

- Pumps and tubing for collecting water samples from specific places

- Sample bottles of different sizes for different types of water samples (The largest bottle is called a carboy.)

- Camera and flash in waterproof boxes for taking pictures underwater

- Laptop computer to connect to instruments such as the camera to collect data

- An instrument called a flow meter to determine how fast the water is flowing

- Coolers with ice to store and cool the samples until they are analyzed at the lab

- A special vacuum that works in air or underwater

- Car batteries to power the pumps and vacuum for sampling

- Thick wading boots to provide some protection from alligators, snakes, and razor-sharp sawgrass

- Mask and snorkel to explore what lies underwater

- Stove, cans of food, water, headlamps, and bug spray to help Laurel and Dan get safely through the night in the Everglades

After a forty-minute ride, the crew arrives at the research station, which is a boardwalk platform built in the middle of the marsh. The driver waves good-bye to Laurel and Dan as they begin to get their equipment organized on the platform. They have a lot to do before the airboat returns to pick them up the next morning.

Dan's first job is to use a scientific instrument called a flow meter to measure how quickly the water is flowing. This is important to know because the flow delivers necessary nutrients and sediment to ecosystems downstream. If the plants and animals downstream don't get the water containing these materials, they'll have trouble surviving.

Laurel puts on her thick wading boots and sloshes through the marsh to measure the height of the squishy soil called **peat** in different places. The height of the peat determines the type of plants that can grow in a certain place and the type of shelter and feeding grounds that animals will find there. Laurel plans to make measurements in a slough habitat, where wading birds like egrets can feast on fish, and in a higher sawgrass ridge habitat, where small fish and shrimp can seek shelter.

Peat: Soil that is made up of decaying pieces of plants and other organisms. Sometimes large masses break away and float on the water surface. Seeds blown by the wind settle on the floating peat, send down roots, and grow into trees that become roosts for wading birds like the white ibis. For some time, these pop-up tree islands continue to float on the surface of the water until eventually they merge with the bottom or other islands.

Even though the air is so hot, Laurel needs to wear long sleeves and pants for walking through the sawgrass. Each blade of grass has rows of teeth like a miniature saw, and Laurel doesn't want to get cut. She is glad she is wearing strong boots when something big and heavy bumps into the side of her foot. Laurel is not sure she wants to know whether the something was a turtle or an alligator. She reminds herself that most gators are afraid of humans and gets on with her work.

After Laurel finishes her peat measurements, she changes into her bathing suit, because her next job is underwater. First, she looks around carefully to make sure there are no alligators nearby. Then she straps on a mask and snorkel and lowers herself into the water to try to see sediment particles in motion. Later she'll set up her special underwater camera to take pictures of the moving particles. But first she wants to see with her own eyes whether the water is flowing fast enough to carry these nutrient-rich particles to plants and animals downstream. Some larger sediment particles called **floc** eventually settle and become part of the peat. Some scientists think that flow needs to scoop floc out of sloughs for the sloughs to stay deep and unclogged. The flow then carries the floc to sawgrass, which needs thick layers of peat to survive.

Floc: Large, puffy material made up of decaying plant material. It sits near the peat surface and is so light and loose that if you try to pick it up, it will flow through your fingers. When parts of the Everglades dry out during the summer, the floc can dry up and become part of the peat, affecting the type of habitat that will be found in years to come.

Under the surface of the water lies a whole different world. Laurel looks down and can barely see a few small particles and bits of algae drifting very slowly—too slowly for a healthy Everglades. Looking up, she sees sunlight filtering through chandeliers of **Utricularia** (you-TRICK-you-LAIR-ee-uh) floating at the surface of the water. Laurel is happy to see the *Utricularia*, which can only survive in very clean, fresh water. That's some good news—at least the water in this spot is healthy!

After Laurel finishes snorkeling, she and Dan hurry to get the equipment ready for their next experiments before nightfall. Almost half of their time before the airboat returns is up! First they cover their faces in nets and coat themselves with bug spray to ward off the swarms of mosquitoes that emerge at dusk and stay out all night.

Next, Laurel sets up a special waterproof camera and flash connected to a laptop computer. Throughout the night, she will take underwater pictures that show how the floc is being carried by the flow of water to help scoop out and build up different parts of the wetland. Dan sets up some pumps and tubing to collect samples of sediment to analyze in the lab. He wants to find out how many nutrients are carried by particles of different sizes.

20

Utricularia, also called bladderwort, is actually a carnivorous, or meat-eating, plant. It has long stems that dangle through the water and are attached to bladders that trap very small animals called *zooplankton*. The traps have hair-like triggers, and when zooplankton brush against them, the trap door of the bladder swings open, sucking the zooplankton and water inside before closing again.

After it gets dark, Laurel and Dan take a quick break to eat and reapply bug spray. They notice a light in the distance, moving in rapid zigzags. What could that light be? Soon they find out. The light, attached to an airboat, heads toward their platform. Laurel and Dan wave their arms to try to stop the boat from coming too close. But the driver doesn't expect other people to be out at this time of night, and he doesn't see them until it's almost too late. He stops quickly, creating waves that rock their platform and shake up their instruments.

The driver cuts his engine and asks if everything is all right. He's holding a long grabber stick called a "gig," which is used for catching frogs. Later he'll sell the frogs to restaurants, or he'll eat them himself.

Once the **"frog gigger"** finds out that Laurel and Dan are scientists working to save the Everglades, he tells them how glad he is to hear it. His way of life, and that of his friends and family, depends on the Everglades having healthy plants and animals and lots of clean water.

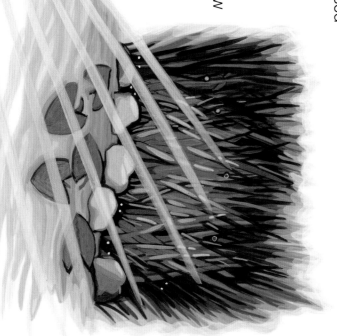

Frog giggers detect frogs by shining their light into the darkness and looking for white eye shine. Alligators' eyes shine brightly when lit by flashlight, too. Large alligators' eyes will glow red, while smaller alligators' eyes glow green.

22

After the frog gigger leaves, the night becomes very quiet and peaceful, except for the constant buzzing of mosquitoes around their face nets. The Milky Way emerges like a million pinpricks of light spilled across the sky, and every so often, a nearby bull alligator bellows loudly.

Laurel yawns and glances at the computer, and suddenly, something huge appears on the screen. She gasps, breaking the silence. The underwater camera had captured a close-up picture of a crayfish in the water, hugely magnifying its claw! In her sleepy state, it had surprised her and looked like something out of a horror movie—not the drifting floc she was hoping to capture on film!

When Laurel looks at the rest of the photos later, she sees that she actually has many photographs of zooplankton and other crayfish, as well. She realizes that the swimming of these creatures may help to stir up the floc so that it can be carried by the current to habitats downstream. This is an important discovery, and she makes sure to note it in her journal.

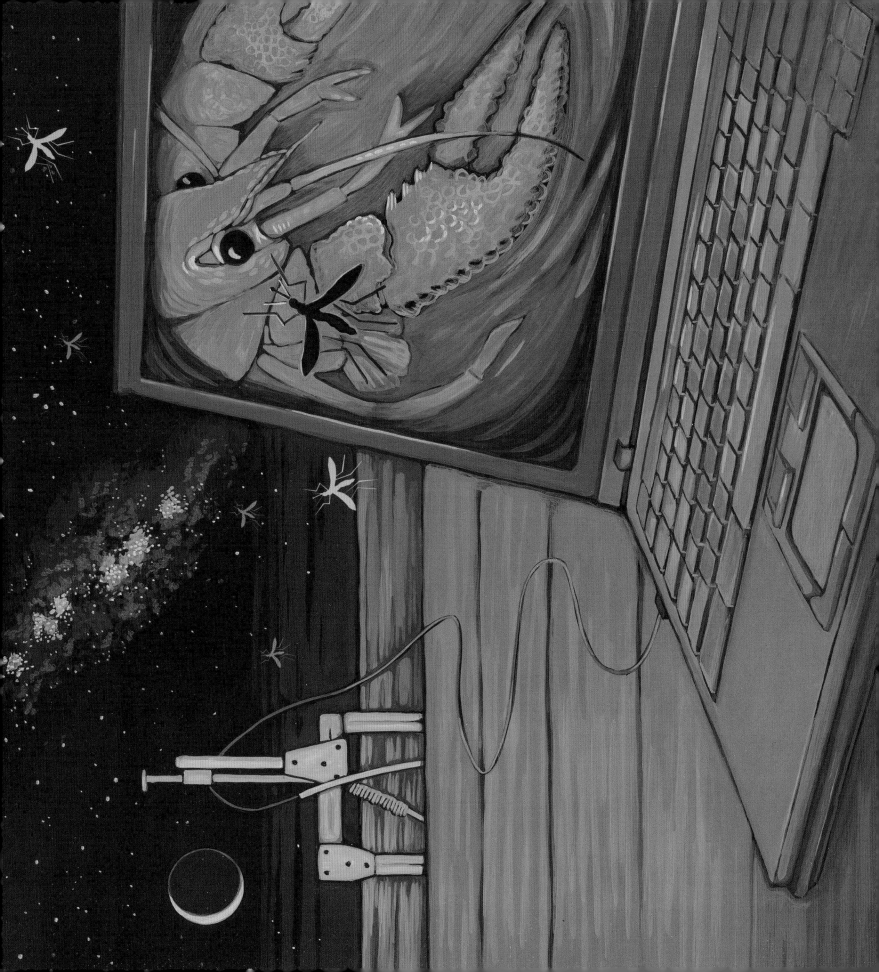

The sunrise begins with a fading of the stars, followed by a pale light in the east that turns the wispy clouds shades of orange and pink. As the whining of the mosquitoes begins to disappear, Laurel can hear the soft wing beats of herons, egrets, and ibises as they fly from their nighttime roosts to their daytime feeding grounds. Laurel and Dan have heavy eyes and are itchy from the mosquito bites that cover their bodies despite their attempts to avoid them. But they know that they must complete one more job before they can go home.

Laurel needs to collect a large amount of floc to study back at the laboratory. There she will be able to figure out just how fast the water must be flowing before it will scoop floc out of sloughs and carry it downstream. Then she will know how fast the water would need to flow in a more natural, restored Everglades. To collect the floc, she climbs back into the water with the hose of the shop vacuum and sucks up masses of fluffy brown floc. She laughs to herself to think that she's using a vacuum cleaner in the Everglades. But she finds that it's much more enjoyable to vacuum floc for a science experiment than to vacuum the rug at home.

Just after Laurel finishes filling the last carboy with floc, the airboat driver returns to take Dan and her home. They load up all of their equipment and head back to the dock, exhausted from their overnight adventure but eager to look at their findings back at the lab. They hope that what they learned during their one night in the Everglades will provide a piece to the puzzle of the Everglades restoration project.

Settled on the boat, Laurel watches the morning sky. She sees a hawk fly overhead and wonders what a hawk might be looking down on in another hundred years. She hopes that it will see panthers prowling in the forest and gators swimming in the sloughs. She hopes there will be **bromeliads** blooming and cypress trees waving. She hopes for clean, flowing water, and for miles and miles of healthy marshes.

Bromeliads: Tropical plants that grow on the trunks or branches of trees instead of in the soil.

28

The restoration of the Everglades still has a long way to go. It is the biggest restoration project ever attempted, and the world is watching south Florida to see if it will be successful. It's important to do what we can to save all the wild areas of the world, whether it's the ice cap of the Arctic, the rain forests of South America, or the Everglades of Florida. Each has something special to offer the world. Preserving the natural wildlife and beauty of these places will be a gift to ourselves and to future generations. You can do your part to conserve water and protect the Earth in simple ways:

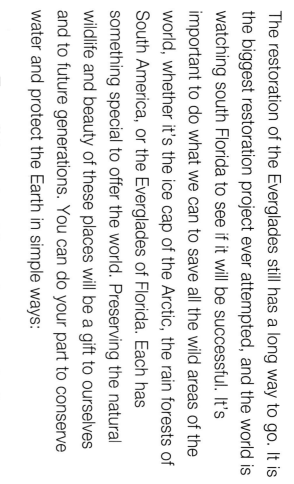

- Turn off the water while you brush your teeth.
- Water your lawn in the early morning, late evening, or at night.
- Take quick showers instead of baths.
- Recycle.
- Fix leaks around your house.

Hopefully you will have the chance to visit the Everglades someday and learn about its unique wildlife and landscapes. Share with your family and friends what you learn. The more people who know about this beautiful natural treasure, the more people there will be working to save it.

LAUREL LARSEN, Ph.D.,

grew up in Titusville, Florida, where she spent much of her time enjoying the outdoors—hiking, kayaking, bicycling, and birdwatching. Although she moved away to Saint Louis, Missouri, for college and then to Boulder, Colorado, for graduate school, her dissertation research on the Everglades ridge and slough landscape took her back to her home state. Currently, Laurel is a research ecologist for the U.S. Geological Survey in Reston, Virginia. She continues to research the Everglades but also studies stream restoration. In her spare time she enjoys bicycle racing and cooking.

JOYCE MIHRAN TURLEY

specializes in presenting images of nature with a painterly style and colorful palette, engaging readers of all ages. Her upcoming and recent works focus on introducing children to the native animals and unique ecosystems of our national parks including Everglades, Grand Canyon, and Glacier. Her bird illustrations appear in award-winning nonfiction books featuring loons and ospreys. Having studied applied mathematics along with fine art, Joyce retired from engineering over 25 years ago to spend time with her family and to pursue her career in illustration. Her technical perspective results in vibrant illustrations with a unique balance of analytic and artistic elements. Raised in upstate New York, Joyce has lived with her husband in the foothills of the Colorado Rockies for over 30 years. Her studio, located in their now "empty nest," permits convenient observation of deer, coyotes, lizards, eagles, and snakes—just outside the picture windows!

RUDOLF JAFFÉ, Ph.D.,

the coordinator for the production of this book, is the George Barley Professor of Environmental Chemistry at Florida International University's Southeast Environmental Research Center (SERC) and a principal investigator of the Florida Coastal Everglades Long Term Ecological Research Program (FCE-LTER). He was responsible for generating the funding that made the production of this book possible and helped coordinate the written and illustrated production. He is indebted to both Laurel Larsen and Joyce Turley for their fantastic contributions and their energy and enthusiasm throughout the production of this book. The financial support through grants from the Hubbard Brook Research Foundation, the SERC Endowment, and supplementary funding through the National Science Foundation to the FCE-LTER made this work possible.

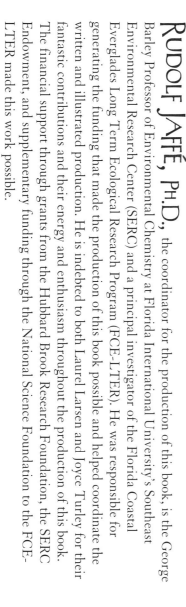

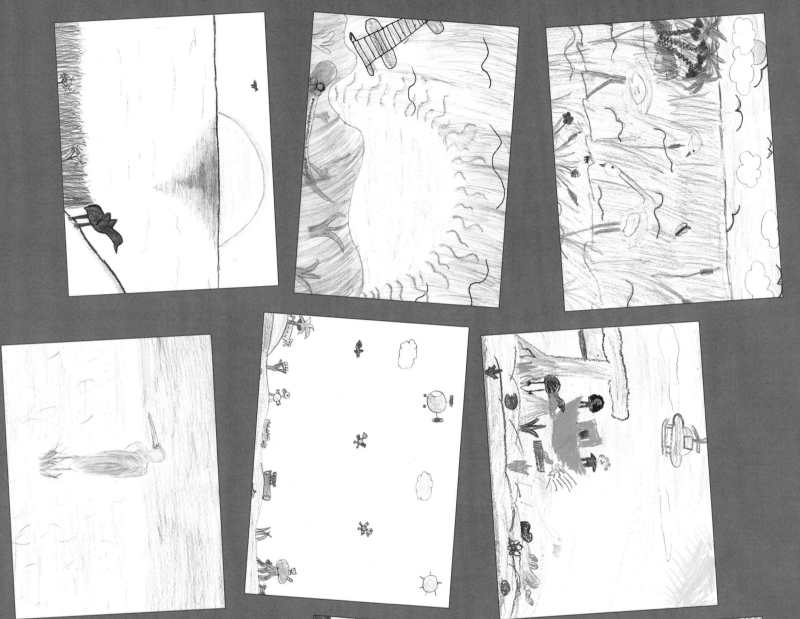